Dear Parent:
Your child's love of reading starts here!

Every child learns to read in a different way and at his or her own speed. Some go back and forth between reading levels and read favorite books again and again. Others read through each level in order. You can help your young reader improve and become more confident by encouraging his or her own interests and abilities. From books your child reads with you to the first books he or she reads alone, there are I Can Read Books for every stage of reading:

SHARED READING
Basic language, word repetition, and whimsical illustrations, ideal for sharing with your emergent reader

BEGINNING READING
Short sentences, familiar words, and simple concepts for children eager to read on their own

READING WITH HELP
Engaging stories, longer sentences, and language play for developing readers

READING ALONE
Complex plots, challenging vocabulary, and high-interest topics for the independent reader

ADVANCED READING
Short paragraphs, chapters, and exciting themes for the perfect bridge to chapter books

I Can Read Books have introduced children to the joy of reading since 1957. Featuring award-winning authors and illustrators and a fabulous cast of beloved characters, I Can Read Books set the standard for beginning readers.

A lifetime of discovery begins with the magical words "I Can Read!"

Visit www.icanread.com for information
on enriching your child's reading experience.

For Sally

HarperCollins®, ✸®, and I Can Read Book® are trademarks of HarperCollins Publishers Inc.

Danny and the Dinosaur Go to Camp Copyright © 1996 by Syd Hoff All rights reserved. No part of this book may be used or reproduced in any manner whatsoever without written permission except in the case of brief quotations embodied in critical articles and reviews. Printed in the United States of America. For information address HarperCollins Children's Books, a division of HarperCollins Publishers, 1350 Avenue of the Americas, New York, NY 10019. www.harpercollinschildrens.com

Library of Congress Cataloging-in-Publication Data
Hoff, Syd, date
    Danny and the dinosaur go to camp / story and pictures by Syd Hoff.
        p.   cm.—(An I can read book)
    Summary: Danny and his friend the dinosaur go to summer camp together.
    ISBN-10: 0-06-026439-X (trade bdg.) — ISBN-13: 978-0-06-026439-0 (trade bdg.)
    ISBN-10: 0-06-026440-3 (lib. bdg.) — ISBN-13: 978-0-06-026440-6 (lib. bdg.)
    ISBN-10: 0-06-444244-6 (pbk.) — ISBN-13: 978-0-06-444244-2 (pbk.)
    [1. Dinosaurs—Fiction. 2. Camps—Fiction.] I. Title. II. Series.
PZ7.H672Dap 1996   95-12410
[E]—dc20   CIP
                                                                                                                    AC

❖

DANNY and the DINOSAUR Go to Camp

story and pictures by
SYD HOFF

HarperCollins*Publishers*

Danny went to camp

for the summer.

He took along his friend

the dinosaur.

"Camp is fun.

You will enjoy it," said Danny.

"Thanks. I needed a vacation,"

said the dinosaur.

6

"Welcome," said the camp owner.
"You're the first dinosaur
we ever had here."

7

Lana the leader said,

"Let's start with a race.

On your mark, get set, go!"

8

The dinosaur took a step.

"You win!" shouted Danny.

The children played football.

The dinosaur ran with the ball,

and nobody could stop him.

"Touchdown!" shouted Danny.

Lana took everybody to the lake.
"Here is where we row our boats,"
she said.

The children rowed little boats.

Danny rowed the dinosaur.

It was time for lunch.

"Please pass the ketchup,"
said Danny.

"Of course, just as soon as
I finish this bottle,"
said the dinosaur.

After lunch
everybody wrote letters home.
"Please send me my own ketchup,"
Danny wrote.

"Send me a pizza,"
wrote the dinosaur.

"Now let's go on a hike,"

said Lana,

and everybody followed her.

Then Danny got tired
and climbed on the dinosaur.

"Wait for us!
We're tired too!"
shouted the children.

"Hold tight," said the dinosaur.

The dinosaur even carried Lana!

It got dark.

Everybody sat around the campfire.

Lana gave out toasted marshmallows.

"Here, have all you want,"

she said.

"Thanks, but I don't have room
for more," said Danny.

"I have room,"
said the dinosaur.

It was time for bed.

"I can't wait to get

under the covers,"

said Danny.

"Me too," said the dinosaur.

But the dinosaur's bunk
was too small for him.

30

He took a pillow
and went outside.

"Wake me up for breakfast,"
said the dinosaur,
and he fell asleep on the ground.
"Good night," Danny said.